Horny Cock Muncher

: The Rise to the Top

Written by: Willie S.

Introduction:

Jean Bolfe was never meant to be just another face in the crowd. He once knew what his future would hold, but reality had other plans—leaving him bouncing at a club in Dublin, Ohio, his degree gathering dust while he wrangled rowdy revelers under neon lights. For years, Jean's life felt stuck in neutral, every shift a replay of the last. But all that changed the night he discovered an invitation to a mysterious eating contest, his first ever, not including the 2 cartons of takeout 2 nights a week while challenging himself, this was a chance to break free, to chase something unexpected and wild. This is the story of how a simple note, a simple suggestion, turned Jean's ordinary nights into an adventure, where he dared to step out of limbo and discover just how far he could go.

Table of Contents

Let's Begin…

Chapter 1: Out of Limbo, I Go

Jean's nights always ended the same way—under neon lights, the buzz of bass trembling through the club walls, the laughter and shouts of partygoers weaving with the throb of electronic music. Tonight, however, felt different, very different and to Jean somehow it would be. The crowd was winding down, the last stragglers gathering their belongings and making their way out into the chilly Dublin night. Jean, with his security vest still zipped, watched them go with a half-smile, nodding to familiar faces. He had become something of a fixture at the club—a steady hand, a quiet presence, someone who could calm a heated argument or help a tipsy regular find their way home.

But beneath the routine, Jean felt a slow tide of restlessness. The job paid the bills, sure, but it had become a holding pattern—a place where his dreams idled, engine running, waiting for a green light that never seemed to come. As the last of the crew clocked out, he gathered his things and headed for the parking lot, the night air cool on his face. He took a deep breath, savoring the silence after hours of cacophony, before sliding into his aging sedan. Tonight, he promised himself, would be different.

On the driver's seat, Jean found a folded slip of paper, yellowed at the edges as if it had been handled many times. He reached for it, eyebrows raised. "Eating contest: Be the cow, join now," it read in blocky handwriting. The message, odd and playful, struck a chord in Jean's imagination. He grinned, picturing himself at a long table, plates stacked high, an audience roaring with every bite. It was a fantasy so far removed from the club's fluorescent monotony that he almost laughed out loud.

He had heard whispers about the contest from a friend—
tales of local legends and wild stories, where ordinary folks
became minor celebrities for a night. For days, the idea had
lingered in his mind, circling like a persistent moth. Now,
with the invitation literally in hand, Jean felt the stir of
possibility. Instead of tossing the note into the glove
compartment, he set it on the dash, glancing again at the
phone number printed below.

Jean had been mulling over the eating contest for several
days now. Each time he glanced at the slip of paper sitting
on his dashboard, the anticipation grew, crowding out the
doubts and hesitations that usually stopped him from
chasing anything new. He hesitated only briefly. The time
for wondering was over; tonight, he would act. This time,
he refused to let hesitation win. With a decisive nod to
himself, he picked up his phone, punched in the number
scrawled on the note, and pressed call.

The line rang just once before a cheerful, professional voice answered, "Hello, you have reached the National Average Eating Contest. Who am I speaking to?" The question hung in the air, and Jean felt his nerves flutter, but he steadied himself. "Hi, this is Jean. I heard about your contest from a friend, and I'd like to enter," he said, his voice betraying a hint of excitement.

"Thank you for calling, Jean," the voice replied with brisk enthusiasm. "Here's what you need to do: visit our website at naec.ie, click the 'Sign Up' button on the homepage, and fill out the entry form. You'll need to provide your full name, contact information, and a brief description of your favorite food. Once you've submitted your entry, you'll receive a confirmation email with event details, including the date, location, and guidelines. If you have any questions, feel free to reach out to our support team. We look forward to seeing you at the contest!" The instructions were clear and easy to follow, leaving little room for uncertainty.

They exchanged polite goodbyes, and Jean hung up, feeling a surge of energy pulse through his chest. Instead of the usual routine—slipping into bed as the city quieted—he made himself a cup of tea and sat down at his battered kitchen table with his laptop. The glow of the screen illuminated his face as he typed "National Average Eating Contest" into the search bar. The homepage burst to life in vivid colors, images of smiling competitors, and towering plates of food.

Jean navigated to the sign-up page, fingers tapping nervously at the keys. He filled out each section with care, pausing when he reached the part about his favorite food. After a moment's thought, he typed "homemade lasagna— a dish that never lets me down." He smiled, remembering all the times he'd helped his grandmother layer noodles and sauce on quiet Sunday afternoons. With a final click, he submitted his entry.

A minute later, a confirmation email arrived in his inbox, complete with a digital ticket and a PDF packet of rules for the event. Jean skimmed the details: competitors would have thirty minutes to eat as much as they could from a rotating menu of classic dishes—burgers, fries, hot dogs, and more. He could almost taste the savory aromas already.

He leaned back in his chair, a deep sense of satisfaction settling over him. He had taken the first real step toward something new, something far from the dim routine of club security shifts and silent car rides home. For the first time in a long while, Jean felt possibility blooming inside him.

But as the initial rush faded, a new thought emerged, glancing at the kitchen counter littered with takeout containers and coffee mugs. The idea of "training" for an eating contest seemed both absurd and thrilling. He grabbed a notepad and started jotting ideas: timing himself with different foods, researching techniques online, maybe even inviting a friend over for a mock contest.

As the evening gave way to quiet, Jean leaned back in his chair, eyes searching the ceiling for inspiration. He knew he'd signed up, but the reality of preparing for an eating contest began to settle in, both exciting and nerve-wracking. "How do I practice?" he said aloud. He scrolled through forums and videos, absorbing tips from seasoned competitors—hydration tricks, pacing strategies, and even stories of legendary eaters.

The challenge felt monumental, but Jean's curiosity pushed him forward. He imagined himself at the contest table, the crowd buzzing, a mountain of food before him. With a laugh, he decided tomorrow would be his first "training" session—he'd fill his cart with all the food he could manage, determined to see just how far he could go. The question of practice was daunting, but for now, the anticipation made him feel more alive than he had in years.

The possibilities spun through his mind as the Dublin, you ask where? Well Dublin, Ohio to be exact, night deepened outside his window. He imagined himself at the contest table, the crowd's energy swelling around him, the clatter of cutlery and laughter filling the room. For now, he was content to savor the adventure ahead, knowing that whatever happened next, he was finally moving forward—one bite at a time.

Chapter 2: Training for Triumph

Morning came quietly for Jean, the soft amber light seeping through his curtains well before his alarm sounded. He woke with a sense of purpose, feeling the weight of his decision settle in as a challenge rather than a burden. The memory of clicking "Submit" on his contest entry lingered, feeding a restless anticipation that pressed him to action. Dublin, Ohio outside still slumbered, but Jean was wide awake, already envisioning the week ahead.

He made his way to the kitchen, pushing aside yesterday's takeout containers to fill the kettle. As steam began to rise, he gathered his scattered notepad and reread last night's scribbles: "practice timing, research techniques, hydrate, mock contest." Each bullet point marked a step toward something bigger—something that felt, for the first time in years, entirely his own.

Jean's resolve hardened as he mapped out his training plan. He would devote two hours each day to preparing his body and mind for the contest's demands. But this wasn't ordinary exercise—this was "advanced eating," a phrase he'd found on a forum and now embraced with a mix of irony and determination. He searched online for competitive eating tips, stumbling upon a world of routines and rituals: stomach expansion workouts, breath control exercises, and endless debates on optimal pacing.

Feeling a strange kinship with those faceless competitors, Jean set out to replicate their methods. He started with water training—chugging glass after glass to stretch his stomach, timing each session and recording his progress. The sensation was uncomfortable, verging on absurd, but Jean pressed on, trusting the advice of the seasoned eaters he'd seen on YouTube. Next came "capacity meals": he'd prepare massive bowls of oatmeal, rice, or pasta, eating as much as he could without rushing, then logging his limits in the notepad.

Some mornings found him at the local gym, not for weights but for deep breathing and core strengthening. He paced through the rows of regulars, feeling out of place but focused. Between sets, he'd visualize himself at the contest table, rhythmically chewing, swallowing, and pushing past the point where most people would stop. Jean felt an odd pride in the discipline these routines required—a satisfaction that grew alongside his stamina.

It wasn't all progress. There were evenings when Jean stared at the ceiling, stomach aching, wondering if this challenge was too much. The contest felt monumental—a test of willpower and endurance that sometimes seemed out of reach. On those nights, he'd scroll through forums, searching for stories of first-timers who had overcome their nerves and doubts. "It's not just about eating," one post read, "it's about proving you can do something crazy, and maybe a little great." Jean repeated that line to himself whenever anxiety crept in.

Work remained a constant backdrop—a steady rhythm of security shifts at the club, late-night drives home, the city's lights blurring past his windshield. Jean tried to fit his training around his job, sipping water between rounds, reading articles during breaks. Some coworkers noticed the change. "Getting into marathon running?" asked Mark, one of the bartenders. Jean grinned, admitting, "Something like that. Just training for a contest." He kept the details vague, worried that telling the full story would invite laughter or disbelief.

Yet, a few nights later, word spread. One of the servers, curious and supportive, offered to help with a mock contest—bringing over a mountain of fries and burgers for Jean to test his limits. The impromptu session was messy, full of laughter and encouragement, reminding Jean that maybe he wasn't as alone in this as he thought.

Midweek, as Jean scrolled through the contest FAQ once more, a detail jumped out at him: "First place prize—$5,000." He read the line twice, feeling a jolt of excitement and uncertainty. Five thousand dollars was more than just prize money; it was possibility. Rent, savings, a fresh start. The thought lingered, bringing a new edge to his motivation. Was it the money he wanted, or the validation of winning? Jean couldn't decide, but he knew he'd give everything for a shot at both.

He wrestled with the question during his late-night drives, imagining what he might do if he won. Would it change anything? Would he still feel that bloom of possibility, or would it fade with the last bite? For now, the answer didn't matter. The contest was his goal, and he was determined to see it through.

The morning of the contest dawned bright and chilly. Jean dressed carefully, choosing a comfortable shirt and loose-fitting jeans—clothes he hoped would serve him well at the table. The event was held in a sprawling convention center, filled with the hum of anticipation and the scent of grilling meat. Rows of long tables stretched across the hall, each set with plates piled high with burgers, fries, hot dogs, and the occasional mountain of lasagna.

Jean arrived early, clutching his digital ticket and the rulebook he'd read a dozen times. The crowd buzzed with excitement—families, seasoned competitors, and curious onlookers mingled in a swirl of voices. The overhead lights cast sharp reflections on the polished floor, making everything feel bigger, brighter, almost surreal.

He scanned the faces around him, noticing the nervous energy that pulsed through the other contestants. Some wore matching T-shirts, others carried lucky charms. Jean felt a flutter in his chest but steadied himself, recalling the hours of training and the encouragement from friends. This was his moment.

The announcer's voice boomed across the room, outlining the contest rules and firing up the crowd. Jean took his seat, hands trembling as the plates were set before him. Thirty minutes, a rotating menu, and one simple goal: eat as much as possible.

He started slow, remembering the advice to pace himself, not to rush the first few bites. The food was good—savory, hot, and abundant. Jean fell into a rhythm: bite, chew, swallow, breathe. With each passing minute, he pushed further, using water to help him swallow, closing his eyes to block out distractions. He felt the struggle build—his stomach protesting, his body demanding he stop. But he pressed on, driven by the cheers of the crowd and the promise of the prize.

Competitors dropped out one by one, some stopping to laugh, others grimacing in defeat. Jean kept going, locking into the zone he'd trained for all week. He drew strength from the memories of quiet afternoons with his grandmother, the discipline of his routines, and the encouragement of those who believed in him.

With only a few minutes left, Jean dug deep, pushing past discomfort. The announcer's countdown echoed in his ears—ten seconds, five, four, three… the bell rang out, and it was done. Jean slumped back in his chair, exhausted, barely able to process what had happened.

The hall erupted as the announcer tallied the plates. "We have a winner—Jeeeeeaaaaannnnnn!" The sound was thunderous, the applause overwhelming. Jean sat stunned, then stood, unsteady on his feet, as the spotlight found him. He managed a shaky bow, heart pounding with pride and disbelief.

The crowd's energy swelled, congratulating him with high fives and cheers. Jean felt lightheaded, a mix of exhaustion and exhilaration flooding his senses. He glanced at the prize table, the promise of $5,000 now more real than ever.

As the adrenaline faded, Jean excused himself and hurried to the bathroom, the reality of the contest catching up to him. He leaned against the cool tile, breathing deeply, letting the magnitude of his achievement settle in, and a magnitude of his food out. This was his first contest, his first win—and he had earned every moment.

Back in the hall, Jean gathered his things, replaying the journey from hesitant beginner to triumphant competitor. The discipline, the doubt, the laughter—all of it had brought him to this point. He thought of the possibilities that lay ahead, the new doors that might open. For now, he was content to savor the victory, knowing that he had chosen courage over comfort, challenge over routine.

~ 21 ~

As the event wound down and the Dublin night deepened, Jean left the convention center with a spring in his step and hope blooming in his heart. The future felt wide open, full of contests yet to come, victories waiting to be claimed— one bite at a time.

Chapter 3: Competing with Friends

Jean sat at his kitchen table one bright March morning, the sun peeking shyly through the window as he stared at a half-eaten bowl of oatmeal. He poked at it with a spoon, still not entirely convinced that "slow carbs" would help a competitive eater. It had been nearly two months since his triumphant win in Dublin, and the taste of victory lingered—alongside a faint ache in his stomach. But what lingered even more was the itch to compete again, to feel the electric surge of adrenaline and the roar of a crowd hungry for spectacle, if not for actual food.

His phone buzzed, interrupting his breakfast musings. A notification lit up: Competitive Eating League—Marquette, Michigan: Hamburger Dog Tag Team Challenge! Jean grinned. Hamburger dogs? He squinted at the screen. The contest rules declared that each team must consist of two eaters, and each "dog" was a hot dog-shaped, grilled hamburger. It sounded like something dreamed up at a summer camp where the chef had lost the will to care about conventional meat shapes.

Jean knew immediately who he'd invite. He dialed Kenneth Trimble, his long-time buddy and noted connoisseur of questionable food combinations. Kenneth answered after a single ring, his voice already booming with enthusiasm.

Jean: "Ken, how do you feel about making history in Marquette? It's a hamburger hot dog contest. They call it 'hamburger dogs'—it's like Frankenstein but for lunch."

Kenneth (laughing): "If it's got bun and meat, you know I'm in. What's the catch? We gotta eat it while juggling chainsaws or something?"

Jean: "No chainsaws. Just buns, hamburger-shaped like hot dogs, and the glory of victory. Team of two. You and me."

Kenneth: "Ate seven hamburgers at your house last summer. Didn't even have a contest. This time, I want a trophy. Or at least a T-shirt that says, 'I survived Jean's competitive eating challenge.'"

They spent the next fifteen minutes riffing on possible team names and training strategies. Kenneth suggested "Bun Believers" and "The Meat Meteors," while Jean pitched "Double Trouble Digestion." They settled on "Team Gut Instinct," a name Kenneth declared "both descriptive and prophetic."

The week before the contest, Jean and Kenneth crammed their duffels with stretchy pants, antacids, and a suspicious number of wet wipes. They drove up to Marquette in Kenneth's dented blue Subaru, the trunk rattling ominously, as if protesting their mission.

Marquette greeted them with a chilly breeze and the scent of pine trees. The contest venue—an old high school gym—was already decked with banners: "Welcome Hamburger Dog Heroes!" The organizers had gone all out, lining the walls with inflatable hot dogs and giant foam burgers. Contestants milled about, some in matching tracksuits, others nervously clutching water bottles. One team wore full hamburger costumes, complete with sesame seed hats.

Kenneth (eyeing costumes): "Jean, why didn't we think of dressing up? Next year, I'm wearing a bun suit. You can be the ketchup."

They registered at the front desk, where a cheerful woman handed them team badges and two coupons for a free milkshake—ostensibly for after the contest, though Kenneth immediately tried to redeem his.

Jean: "Ken, save it for the victory lap. If you drink that now, they'll need a mop before the contest even starts."

Kenneth (winking): "It's called carbo-loading, my friend. Or dairy-loading. Or just loading."

In the hours before the contest, teams gathered in the corner gym to "warm up." Jean and Kenneth sat at a plastic table, strategizing while Kenneth demonstrated his "jaw stretch" by repeatedly popping his jaw and making faces at passing competitors.

Kenneth: "You know, Jean, if we eat fast enough, maybe the judges won't notice we're chewing. Just inhale, like a vacuum."

Jean: "That's not a strategy, that's a hospital visit waiting to happen."

They watched as another team practiced by wolfing down breadsticks. The duo in hamburger costumes attempted synchronized eating to the beat of "Eye of the Tiger" blaring from a tinny speaker. One of them choked, coughed, and gave a thumbs-up.

Kenneth: "We should've brought theme music. I vote for 'Hungry Eyes.'"

Jean: "I'm more of a 'Don't Stop Believin'' kind of guy. Especially when the buns start stacking up."

The bell rang, and the contestants took their places at long tables, each lined with platters of hamburger dogs—thick, hot dog-shaped burgers nestled in fluffy buns, topped with mustard and ketchup squiggles. The aroma was formidable, a heavy, greasy cloud that lingered like a challenge.

The MC—a man with a microphone shaped like a pickle—introduced each team. When "Team Gut Instinct" was called, Jean and Kenneth rose, flexed their "eating arms" in unison, and bowed to the crowd. Kenneth blew a kiss to the judges, earning a confused look and a few giggles.

Kenneth (whispering): "If I go down, tell my mom I loved her. And tell my stomach I'm sorry."

Jean: "You'll be fine. If you pass out, I'll finish your share. That's teamwork."

The timer started, and plates were passed down the line. Jean took the first bite, the juicy meat almost too hot. Kenneth immediately began narrating his process, loud enough for the first several rows of spectators.

Kenneth: "First, you wanna angle the bun—like so—then you compress, maximize intake, minimize chewing. It's science, folks!"

A nearby competitor, a wiry man named Troy with a handlebar mustache, leaned over and said, "If I eat more than you, do I get those milkshake coupons?" Kenneth grinned, ketchup smeared across his cheek.

Kenneth: "If you eat more than me, I'll buy you a milkshake and personally perform 'Eye of the Tiger' in interpretive dance."

Jean nearly choked laughing, but managed to stay focused, remembering his Dublin discipline—bite, chew, swallow, breathe. The crowd cheered, chanting team names and waving inflatable hamburger bats.

Twenty minutes in, the heat was on—literally. The hamburger dogs had cooled, but Kenneth was sweating like a marathon runner. He waved at the judges for water, accidentally knocking a bun off the table.

Kenneth (panicking): "Bun down! We've got a bun casualty!"

Jean, meanwhile, found a rhythm—two bites per dog, quick sip, repeat. He stole glances at Kenneth, who was now humming the theme to "Rocky" and occasionally flapping his arms.

Jean (smirking): "You're not a bird, Ken. Stop flapping."

Kenneth (gasping): "If I believe I'm lighter, maybe I'll digest faster. It's quantum physics. Maybe."

A rogue bun rolled under the table and hit the sneaker of a judge. He peered down and announced, "Buns are not for the floor, gentlemen!" The crowd erupted in laughter.

Troy, the mustachioed competitor, attempted to intimidate them by stuffing two hamburger dogs at once, cheeks bulging. Kenneth responded by serenading him with a muffled rendition of "Hungry Eyes."

As the contest neared its climax, the competitors' faces revealed a mix of determination and regret. Jean wiped mustard from his chin, steeling himself for the last round, while Kenneth stared dramatically into the crowd, clutching his stomach like a Shakespearean actor facing his final act. The emcee ramped up the energy, counting down the final seconds as everyone braced for one last, unforgettable bite.

As the emcee's countdown hit zero, a hush fell over the crowd, punctuated only by the sound of ketchup bottles collapsing and the distant wheeze of someone's grandma fanning herself with a scorecard. Contestants slumped back in their seats, bellies taut, eyes glazed over. Jean and Kenneth sat side by side, their plates cleared, their expressions a chaotic blend of pride and mild distress.

The head judge, still nursing a bruised shin from the rogue bun incident, stood and tapped the microphone. "Ladies and gentlemen, we have tallied the crumbs, counted the bites, and conferred with the bun integrity committee." He paused, watching as Kenneth squinted up at the sky, perhaps hoping for a sign from the meat gods. "It is my honor to announce… the winners of this year's Hamburger Dog Duel—Jean and Kenneth!"

The audience exploded into applause. Kenneth managed a fist pump, nearly toppling backward off his chair. Jean, ever the picture of composure, tried to stand, only to discover his legs had temporarily decided to unionize and refuse all further labor. He gripped the table, grinning at Kenneth.

Kenneth (hoarse, heroic): "We did it, Jean. We stared down the beefy abyss—and the abyss blinked first."

Jean (wincing): "Speak for yourself. My stomach just filed for witness protection."

The emcee, sporting a dazzling bow tie and an even more dazzling smile, ushered the champions forward. He handed them a trophy shaped suspiciously like a hamburger dog— complete with tiny sesame seed details and a removable mustard cap. Kenneth promptly tried to unscrew the cap, convinced there was a real condiment inside.

Photographers swarmed the stage, shouting for the winners to "look hungry!" and "give us your best post-meat face!" Jean managed a thumbs-up while Kenneth, ever the showman, attempted a victory dance. It was mostly a wobbly shuffle, part interpretive jazz, part "my shoelaces are tied together."

Meanwhile, Troy—the mustachioed rival—approached, clutching his own consolation prize: a giant, inflatable ketchup bottle. He offered a grudging nod. "Not bad, fellas. Next year, I bring the spicy relish."

Jean extended a hand, which Troy shook—using only two fingers, presumably still sticky with condiments. Kenneth clapped Troy on the back with such enthusiasm that a stray pickle slice shot from someone's plate and landed in the trophy's mustard reservoir.

The crowd chanted their names, and the judges presented them with sashes that read, "Lord of the Dogs" and "Baron von Bun." Kenneth wore both, insisting that one was for him and the other for his digestive tract. Jean just rolled his eyes and accepted a celebratory bottle of antacid from a local pharmacist.

As they posed for one last photo, Jean leaned over and whispered, "Next year, we're eating salad." Kenneth grinned. "Only if it's deep-fried and shaped like a dog."

With that, the champions took a bow—well, a seated bow—and basked in the glory of their victory, their stomachs full, their hearts happy, and their futures forever changed by the power of the mighty hamburger dog.

Chapter 4: Taking on Some More Training

Jean sat at the kitchen table, staring at the leftovers from yesterday's epic hamburger dog victory. His stomach was still negotiating peace talks, but his mind raced with fresh ambition. The taste of triumph lingered not just on his palate, but in his soul. Winning "Lord of the Dogs" was fun, but the appetite for greatness—along with sixty-five milligrams of antacid—rumbled in his gut. Fame, fortune, and the lure of starring in a commercial for "Mega Mustard" danced before him like golden french fries in a deep fryer. The next big eating contest was coming up in Lafayette, Louisiana, and the $50,000 prize beckoned him like a siren song composed entirely of sizzling bacon.

Jean knew the stakes were higher than ever. This wasn't just about cramming more hot dogs down his gullet; it was about stepping onto the world stage of competitive eating and gulping down glory. If he was going to compete with the best, he had to prepare like the best. Competitive eating, he realized, was less about reckless jaw action and more about strategic endurance, mental fortitude, and—surprisingly—a touch of artistry. He wanted to train like an Olympian, swapping the track for the table, the hurdles for the hot dogs.

The decision came to him in a moment of clarity—possibly induced by a sugar rush from half a dozen jelly donuts. If Olympic athletes had coaches, why shouldn't competitive eaters? Jean scoured the internet for experts, dodging ads for "Stomach Stretchers" and "Chew Like a Champ" until he found the holy grail: Coach Maggy "The Maw" McAllister, a legend famous for her three-minute taco demolition and her trademarked "Zen of Chew" philosophy.

Their first meeting was less Rocky and more "Rocky Road"—held at Maggy's training studio, which looked suspiciously like a repurposed pie shop. Maggy greeted Jean with a handshake so firm his wrist popped, then scanned him up and down. "You want to eat like an Olympian, kid? You're gonna train like one. Say goodbye to amateur hour."

Maggy wasted no time. "First rule of competitive eating: Respect your body. Second rule: Don't get ketchup on the training mats." Jean's days soon followed a rigorous schedule that would make a triathlete weep:

- Jawercises: Jean wore a weighted mouthpiece and chewed giant licorice ropes until his jaw ached. "Strong jaws win titles," Maggy said, tossing him a beef stick like a baton.
- Stomach Stretches: Every morning, Jean practiced water chugging—gulping pitchers to expand his

stomach capacity. Sometimes he felt like a human aquarium; Kenneth made fish faces to cheer him on.

- Speed Swallow Drills: Coach timed him as he downed mini bagels, racing the clock like a sprinter against the finish line.

- Bite Technique: "You need precision," Maggy insisted, teaching him the art of the side-bite, the bun fold, and the elusive "meat tuck."

- Mental Preparation: Guided meditation playlists filled his earbuds, featuring motivational munching mantras: "You are one with the bun. The bun is one with you."

- Diet Discipline: Jean traded junk food for lean proteins, vegetables, and—ironically—a lot of salad. "It's not just about cramming calories," Maggy lectured. "It's about stamina."

Each day was a blend of sweat, laughter, and the occasional burp. Maggy drilled him on portion control and breathing techniques, even setting up a mock competition complete with cheering sound effects. "Visualize the crowd! Hear the roar!" she shouted as Jean powered through a plate of synthetic chicken nuggets. The first time he reached his personal best, Kenneth hoisted a foam finger and declared him "Most Likely to Swallow the World."

Jean quickly discovered that competitive eating was as much a psychological contest as it was a physical one. Every morning, as he rubbed his aching jaw and stretched his sore midsection, he found himself wondering if he had bitten off more than he could chew—literally and figuratively. Maggy's relentless regimen pushed his body to new limits, but what surprised him most was how much his mind resisted.

The physical hurdles were constant and varied. Chugging pitchers of water left Jean feeling bloated, sometimes sick; the sensation of his stomach stretching was both alarming and necessary. There were days when he could barely look at a glass of water without his insides protesting. Yet, the clock was always ticking, and Maggy's whistle signaled the start of yet another round of mouth-stretching and speed swallowing.

Yet, for all the discomfort, it was the mental battles that proved most daunting. The pressure to improve, to keep up with Maggy's high expectations and his own ambitions, weighed on him. During drills, his mind sometimes wandered to thoughts of failure—of choking onstage, or simply not measuring up. The crowd noises Maggy piped in for practice, meant to motivate, occasionally fed his anxiety instead. "You have to want it more than you fear it," Maggy would say, clapping him on the back hard enough to set his teeth rattling.

Chapter 5: Quitting the Job

Jean's decision to quit the bouncer job came on a Thursday morning, after a long shift filled with drunken arguments and a bruised knuckle he didn't remember earning. He stared at his reflection in the club's flickering bathroom light, face puffy from lack of sleep, jaw still aching from last night's swallowing drills. There was a moment—a faint, trembling pause—where he weighed the comfort of a steady paycheck against the fierce pull of the contest circuit. It wasn't just about money anymore. Maggy's voice echoed in his mind: "You have to want it more than you fear it." So he scrawled his resignation on a napkin, left it tucked behind the cash register, and walked away from the world of velvet ropes and neon lights.

He felt lighter, unburdened and terrified. The practicalities snapped at his heels: rent, groceries, the empty fridge. But beneath the anxiety, there was exhilaration. The world of competitive eating offered no guarantees, no safe bets. There were highs—a trophy here, a local headline there—and lows, too: losses that stung, nights spent replaying every misstep. Jean had entered his third year in the circuit as a "lower champion," a title that meant respect among the regulars but little recognition beyond the boardwalks and county fairs. He'd won modest purses and lost to legends, tasted defeat and victory in equal measure. But from now on, there was no fallback; eating was no longer a sideline, but the main event.

Adapting to this new life was like stepping onto a carousel that never stopped spinning. The training, once squeezed between shifts, now dominated his days. Each morning began with Maggy's regimen: speed swallow drills in the cramped kitchen, bite technique reviews with a half-eaten baguette, guided meditation to quiet the lurking doubts. Even his diet had changed—no more bar food, but endless plates of salad, lean protein, and the occasional practice

bagel. Jean's body transformed; so did his mind. Some

days, he awoke feeling invincible, muscles taut, jaw strong.

Other mornings, he questioned everything, rubbing his sore

midsection and wondering if he had bitten off more than he

could chew, both literally and figuratively.

The contest in Lafayette, Louisiana, where Jean is

originally from and has moved back to, loomed as the

season's big test—a regional event with higher stakes and

louder crowds. Lafayette was a city drenched in summer

heat, its streets alive with laughter and the scent of frying

batter. The venue, a converted warehouse, pulsed with

anticipation. Banners flapped overhead, announcing the

"Third Annual Chicken Fried Chili Dog Showdown."

Spectators filed in, clutching paper trays piled high with the

day's signature dish. The air buzzed with excitement,

tinged by friendly wagers and the spicy tang of chili.

Jean arrived early, heart pounding behind his ribs. He scoped out the stage: twelve contestants, each seated at a long table, stacks of chicken fried chili dogs glistening before them. The dogs themselves were a marvel—savory, deep-fried, smothered in thick, peppery chili. The smell alone made his mouth water and his stomach tense. He found his spot, set down his water pitcher, and ran his fingers along the edge of the table, grounding himself.

Pre-competition nerves wove through the crowd and the contestants alike. Jean closed his eyes, letting the chaos fade, recalling Maggy's training. "You are one with the bun. The bun is one with you." He remembered her whistle, her foam finger, the drills that had left him sweating and burping, the mock competitions with piped-in crowd noise. He smiled, letting the memories steady him. He had endured the bloating, the stretching, the days when water itself felt like a foe. Now, he had to channel that discomfort into focus.

As the announcer's booming voice kicked off the contest, Jean started slow. He'd learned that rushing at the outset could spell disaster; stamina was key. The first few bites were measured: side-bite, bun fold, the careful tuck of sausage beneath chili. His jaw worked at a practiced pace, mechanical yet mindful. All around him, the other eaters tore into their plates—some reckless, some methodical. Jean held back, eyes darting to the clock, reading every second.

Within minutes, the initial adrenaline faded and the real battle began. The chili dogs, so delectable at first, became a mass of heat and dough, each bite heavier than the last. Jean's throat burned, his stomach stretched, a familiar ache radiated through his jaw. He remembered Maggy's mantra about portion control and breathing, letting each swallow settle before the next. Sweat pooled on his brow, but he kept pushing. The crowd's cheers grew louder, a wave of sound that crashed with every mouthful.

Halfway through, Jean felt the drag—the subtle shift when the body protests, when the mind wants to quit. He looked out at the audience, found the faces cheering, the foam fingers raised in encouragement. He thought of the nights training in solitude, the sacrifices, the leap he'd made quitting the club. He focused on the rhythm: bite, chew, swallow, breathe. The taste faded to routine, pain dulled by determination. Maggy's voice lingered: "Visualize the crowd! Hear the roar!" And he did.

Then, from the corner of his eye, Jean noticed a competitor pulling ahead: Dave Snapps, a newcomer with a sharp look and an energy that bordered on frantic. Dave attacked his plate with reckless abandon, each chili dog vanishing in seconds. Unlike Jean's calculated approach, Dave seemed driven by something else—a hunger for victory that blazed in his eyes. They locked glances for a moment, a silent challenge exchanged. Jean recognized the look: not just ambition, but the need to prove something, to win it all at any cost.

The tension between them grew, feeding into the atmosphere. The crowd sensed it, shifting their focus from the mass of competitors to the two front-runners. Jean felt his competitive streak flare, not out of malice, but from the thrill of rivalry. He pushed through the discomfort, drawing on every trick Maggy had taught him. He adjusted his breathing, counted his swallows, and upped his pace. The stadium noise became a blur, drowned out by the pounding of his own heart.

With five minutes left, Dave made a move, grabbing two dogs at once, forcing them down in a show of bravado. Jean steadied himself, refusing to be rattled. He switched tactics—focusing on smaller bites, faster swallows. The final stretch was a blur: sweat dripping, hands shaking, the taste of chili and fried batter mingling with adrenaline. The pain was immense, but so was the exhilaration. The crowd stood, shouting encouragements, some chanting Jean's name.

As the final seconds ticked away, every sound seemed to melt into a dull roar—Jean could feel the weight of each bite, the strain in his jaw, but also an odd sense of clarity, a tunnel vision that cut through the pain and the pressure. The last chili dog hovered inches from his lips as the buzzer blared, and with a final, determined swallow, he finished strong, hands trembling but victorious. The judge's whistle blew, confetti drifted down, and the crowd exploded, their cheers nearly shaking the rafters of the old warehouse. Dave Snapps, slick with sweat and breathing hard, shot Jean a grudging nod of respect—rivalry acknowledged, if not yet settled. Maggy rushed forward from the sidelines, foam finger waving, her grin wide enough to light up the entire city. In that moment, with the savory taste of victory and chili still lingering, Jean realized he hadn't just survived another contest—he'd claimed his place at the table, not just as a competitor but as a contender, ready for whatever challenges the next season might bring.

Chapter 6: New Horizons, New Hungers

The confetti from Lafayette still clung to Jean's shoes as he slipped through the crowd, Maggy's voice echoing behind him—half whistle, half war cry. The warehouse air was thick with victory and chili, but already Jean felt something shifting inside, a hunger not just for food but for horizons. That night, sprawled across a hotel bed littered with empty water bottles and crumpled napkins, Maggy broached the next chapter.

"You're bigger than Louisiana, kid. Heck, you're bigger than the South," she declared, brandishing a fold-out map as if it were a golden ticket. "Euro season's heating up. Istanbul's calling, and they want to see what a Cajun can do with lamb."

Jean blinked at the city's name, the unfamiliar syllables rolling off Maggy's tongue. Turkey was a world away from the fried comfort of home, but the thought sparked something wild and electric in his chest. He was no longer just surviving these contests—he was hungry for the world.

Two weeks later, they were on a predawn shuttle to the airport, duffel bags slung low and hearts pounding. Maggy had packed with precision—protein bars, electrolyte powders, and a playlist loaded with crowd noises and motivational mantras. Jean gripped his passport with sweaty hands, laughing as Maggy snapped their selfie under the blinking "Departures" sign.

The flight was a blur of engine hums and half-slept dreams. Somewhere over the Atlantic, Jean stared out the window, the clouds below stretching endless and white. Maggy, ever the coach, jabbed at her phone, reading out facts about Turkish cuisine. "Lamb's leaner than beef. You'll need to chew smarter, not harder. And the spices—they go heavy on cumin and sumac. Imagine chili with perfume!" She mimed a chef's flourish, and Jean grinned, nerves and anticipation mingling.

When they landed, Istanbul hit them like a sun-warmed wave: the call to prayer rising above traffic noise, vendors hawking roasted chestnuts, the Bosphorus shimmering between continents. Jean inhaled the city's energy—sweet, smoky, teeming with histories he barely knew. Street food stalls spilled over with simit rings, sizzling kebabs, and unfamiliar pastries. Maggy sampled everything, taking notes, snapping photos, and pulling Jean into the swirl.

They rode trams through neighborhoods where cats lounged on ancient stones and neon signs blinked in languages Jean couldn't read. He watched Maggy negotiate with street cooks, her hands painting stories in the air. "This is research," she insisted. "You need to know the taste to beat the taste."

Meals became lessons. Lamb, slow-cooked and rolled in flatbread, arrived doused in yogurt and herbs. Jean learned to savor unfamiliar textures, to let the flavors linger. Maggy quizzed him after every bite: "What's the spice? Which part is toughest to chew? How's your jaw holding up?" They laughed over mispronounced dishes and spicy mouthfuls that set his tongue alight.

Their rented flat near the contest venue became a training camp. Maggy taped motivational slogans on the fridge— "Visualize the Finish," "Chew with Purpose," "Breathe the Win." She orchestrated mock contests with local hot dogs, counting Jean's swallows, timing his bites, and blasting Turkish pop music for crowd effect.

Sometimes, homesickness pressed in—Jean missed the fried batter aroma and the familiar holler of Southern crowds. But Maggy's energy never faltered. She'd wake him at dawn for brisk walks along the Spice Bazaar, narrating stories of legendary eaters and surprise upsets. "Remember, the world's full of new flavors and new rivals. You're here to learn, not just to win."

Jean marveled at her intensity. Maggy was equal parts pumper and drill sergeant, her encouragement as sharp as her critiques. She pushed him to study not just food, but his competitors. They watched past contest footage, analyzing techniques—the two-handed bun squeeze, the water dunk, the lightning-fast swallow. "You're not just up against the clock, kid. You're up against history."

In quiet moments, Jean reflected on their evolving partnership. Maggy was no longer simply his coach—she was his tether, his strategist, the steady metronome in the chaos of competition. She knew when to push and when to pull back, reading his moods and limits with uncanny precision. Sometimes, they fell into easy laughter over

Turkish coffee; other times, tension sparked as they debated tactics.

But underlying it all was trust—a sense that together, they could take on whatever strange, spicy, or daunting challenge lay ahead. Maggy's faith in him became his anchor, her drive infectious. She saw possibilities when Jean saw only obstacles, and her belief propelled him forward.

Contest day dawned crisp and clear. The European Eating Championships bustled with a patchwork of competitors— Polish pierogi prodigies, French baguette biters, German bratwurst champions. The venue, a riverside pavilion draped in blue and gold banners, thrummed with anticipation. Local press hovered, snapping photos of the American upstart and his fiery coach.

Backstage, Jean's nerves danced. The Turkish lamb hot dogs, lined up under heat lamps, looked both inviting and intimidating. Their aroma was richer, more complex than anything he'd faced before—a blend of lamb, garlic, and wood smoke. Maggy pressed a cold bottle of water into his palm, her eyes sparkling with challenge. "Remember Lafayette. Remember why you're here. No matter how strange it feels, you belong."

As organizers called the roll, Jean glanced at the international field—a Russian with hands like shovels, a wiry Swede bouncing on his toes. He smiled, nerves melting into resolve. He had come a long way from club nights and chili dog showdowns. Each new competitor was both rival and teacher, each new food a test of will and adaptability.

Minutes before the contest, Maggy led him through breathing drills, her voice steady amidst the hubbub. "Find your center. The bun is different, the crowd is different, but you're still you. Focus on the rhythm: bite, chew, swallow, breathe."

The crowd—louder, more multilingual than back home—pressed in, their shouts a tapestry of encouragement and curiosity. Jean felt their energy, not as pressure, but as possibility. He was about to test himself on the biggest stage yet, and he was ready.

As the emcee counted down in Turkish and English, Jean squeezed Maggy's hand. They were a team forged in sweat, spice, and stubbornness, facing the unknown together. The air crackled with anticipation, and for the first time, Jean felt not just nerves but excitement—a hunger that reached beyond the table, into the heart of the world.

He glanced at the crowd, at Maggy's encouraging grin, and the waiting mountain of lamb hot dogs. This was more than a contest. It was a journey—one that had carried him from fried batter and foam fingers to the banks of the Bosphorus.

Win or lose, he belonged here, ready to claim his place

among the world's best.

Chapter 7: Does She Love Me or the Food?

The riverside pavilion was empty now, but the air still hummed with the ghostly echoes of cheers and multilingual shouts. Blue and gold banners fluttered gently in the dusk as magenta and saffron spilled across the Turkish sky, reflected in the slow-moving Bosphorus. Jean leaned against a sun-warmed railing, his championship badge still dangling askew from his neck, and tried to slow his pounding heart—not from the contest, but from the way Maggy looked at him in the fading light.

The European Eating Championships were over. The Polish pierogi prodigy had wept tears of oniony defeat, a French baguette biter had thrown his beret in disgust, and Jean had finished a respectable third, his stomach stretched, his pride intact. The crowd's energy still buzzed through his veins like strong Turkish coffee. But as the crowd thinned and the riverside emptied, it was Maggy's hand in his that made everything feel electric.

"Are you sure you don't want another lamb hot dog?" Maggy teased, her eyes dancing. She nudged him with her hip, causing the championship badge to swing. "You looked like you were falling in love with them out there."

Jean groaned, clutching his belly. "If I see another lamb hot dog, I'll start speaking fluent Turkish just to beg for mercy."

She laughed—a sound bright and bubbling, more effervescent than the lemonade in his trembling hand. The contest had left them both flushed: Jean from exertion, Maggy from pride and adrenaline. But now, with the sun stretching long shadows and the city's call to prayer curling through the air, something softer crept in.

They found a bench beneath a willow tree, its branches trailing like a curtain. Maggy swung her legs up and leaned into him, her head resting on his shoulder. For a moment, the world stilled. The contest, the crowd, the nerves— everything faded, and it was just them, listening to the gentle lap of water and the distant clatter of a ferry.

"You know," Jean began, "when the emcee counted down, all I could think was, 'If I lose, will she still want to coach me?' And maybe... will she still want to kiss me if I smell like garlic and lamb for a week?"

Maggy grinned and pecked his cheek. "I'll risk it if you will."

The romantic spell broke when Maggy's stomach rumbled—loudly. They burst into laughter, doubled over on the bench.

"See?" Jean declared triumphantly. "You're just jealous you didn't get to eat any of the hot dogs. Maybe you love the food more than me."

Maggy sat up, crossing her arms in mock indignation. "Excuse me! At least when I eat, I don't make faces like someone's wrestling an octopus."

Jean gasped, feigning insult. "That was a look of intense concentration! You try stuffing twelve lamb dogs in six minutes and not making weird faces."

"Maybe I will," she shot back, and before he could protest, she marched to the nearest food stand and bought two more lamb hot dogs. She handed him one with a flourish, a challenge in her eyes. "Rematch right here, right now. Loser owes the winner a foot massage."

They squared off, hot dogs in hand, making an elaborate show of stretching, rolling their shoulders, and counting down in Turkish and English—drawing stares from a passing family and a giggle from a street vendor. Maggy took one dainty bite, then another, chewing exaggeratedly slowly.

"Cheating!" Jean cried. "You're savoring it!"

"I'm appreciating the cultural experience," she replied with a prim air. "You could learn a thing or two."

Their contest ended in fits of laughter and a mess of breadcrumbs, neither able to finish their food through the giggles. Jean brushed a crumb from Maggy's lip, and for a heartbeat, the world spun only for the two of them.

But as the laughter faded, a different mood settled. Maggy tucked her knees under her chin, her expression thoughtful.

"Jean," she said quietly, "can I ask you something? Do you think… do you think you can be good at this—at competing—if we're… you know, together?" She hesitated, fiddling with the sleeve of his jacket. "What if I'm distracting you? What if we're too close, and you can't focus?"

He blinked, surprised. "Distracting? Maggy, you're the reason I made it this far. You see stuff I can't. You push me forward. You're my... coach," he said, stumbling over the word, "but you're also... more."

She bit her lip, looking unconvinced. "But what if your heart's in the wrong place? What if you start eating to impress me, or worse—what if you win, and people say it's just because you're in love with your coach?"

Jean took a deep breath, recalling her words backstage: No matter how strange it feels, you belong. He reached for her hand, threading his fingers through hers.

"Maggy, you make me better. Not just at eating, but at being brave. I could eat a thousand hot dogs and never feel as full as I do when you believe in me. And… if I have to

choose between winning and having you in my corner? I'll

take you, every time."

Chapter 8: Is It All Gone

The sun had begun its slow descent over Istanbul, casting a golden hue on the Bosphorus and the city's distant spires. The festival crowds were thinning, the scent of grilled meats and spices fading on the air, replaced by the hush that settles once the spotlight has shifted elsewhere. In this quiet aftermath, Maggy and Jean found themselves drifting away from the contest grounds—away from the noise, the laughter, and the sting of defeat that lingered like smoke in their chests.

Their hands hung by their sides, no longer entwined. Maggy's sneakers scuffed the ancient cobblestones, her gaze fixed on the ground, counting cracks, a rhythm to anchor her tumbling thoughts. Jean kept a step behind, shoulders tense, jaw tight, the raucous cheers of the crowd still echoing in his mind, now tainted by the image of Dave

Snapps—grinning, victorious, arms raised in triumph. The loss felt raw, not just because of the contest, but because of everything that had led them here.

They walked in silence, only the city's distant bustle filling the quiet between them. When they reached a low stone wall overlooking the water, Maggy stopped. She hugged her knees to her chest, curling inward, as if trying to make herself small enough to disappear. Jean leaned against the wall, watching the ferries cut across the water, searching for words that wouldn't sting.

The contest had ended hours ago, but the result still pressed on both of them—a weight that had nothing to do with the hot dogs or the roaring crowd. Maggy's mind replayed the final moments, Dave Snapps catching up to Jean bite for bite, the glint in Dave's eye, the subtle nod Maggy had given when she'd spotted Dave in the crowd days before.

She'd known he was coming, but hadn't told Jean. That secret now burned her from the inside out.

Maggy broke the silence first, her voice barely above a whisper. "I'm sorry, Jean." She stared at her sneakers, knuckles white where she clung to her legs. "I should have done more. Or... I should have told you. About Dave."

Jean didn't answer. He wanted to say it wasn't her fault, that Dave's win was just part of the game. But doubt lingered, sharp and insistent. He remembered the way Maggy had watched Dave in the qualifying rounds, the way she'd seemed distracted—torn, even—during their last strategy session. Did she want this for him as much as she'd said? Or had she always been rooting for someone else, for the spectacle, for the drama?

Guilt twisted deeper in Maggy's chest. "I'm the reason you lost. I—I let us get too close, didn't I? I made it about us, about feelings, when it was supposed to be about you winning." Her eyes filled with tears, but she blinked them away, determined not to add weakness to her list of faults. "I just… I don't know how to make it right."

Jean's heart ached as he listened. He remembered the thrill of their early days together—the way Maggy's enthusiasm had pulled him out of his own head, the way she had believed in him when he doubted himself. But now, as he watched her struggle with her own doubts, a seed of suspicion took root. Had she come for the fame, the food, the thrill of the scene? Or was it something deeper?

He tried to read her expression, searching for the Maggy he knew—the one who made him laugh, who matched his competitive spirit, who'd become more than just a coach. But all he saw was pain and uncertainty. He hesitated, voice rough. "Did you want Dave to win? Is that why you didn't tell me he was here?"

Maggy shook her head fiercely. "No. I wanted you to win, Jean. I always did. I just… I got scared. I thought maybe if I kept Dave a secret, you'd focus on what you do best. I was wrong. I was selfish." She choked on the word, shame coloring her cheeks. "And now, I've messed everything up."

The memory of Dave's journey flickered between them. After his early exit last season, Dave had clawed his way back through every regional competition, eating his way past legends and newcomers alike. His presence in Turkey felt almost inevitable—a storm gathering on the horizon. Maggy had seen him in the crowd before the semifinals, his eyes locked on Jean, a silent challenge. She'd kept her distance, unsure whether telling Jean would fire him up or throw him off.

Now, Dave's victory hung over Jean like a shadow—a reminder that even the best could be toppled, that every champion was only as strong as his weakest moment. And for Jean, that moment had come when his heart had tangled with Maggy's.

Maggy finally looked at Jean, her eyes searching his. "I should go," she said softly. "We've gotten too close, and it's hurting you. You need to focus on being the competitor you were before I got in the way."

Jean took her hand, his grip gentle but firm. "Don't say that," he murmured. "You didn't get in the way. You made me better. But maybe… maybe I wanted to show off, to prove myself to you, not just for the win. Maybe I got lost in us."

Maggy smiled, sad but sincere. "Me too. I thought coaching you was about pushing you to win. But somewhere along the way, I started hoping you'd notice me, not just my advice. I started putting you ahead of the game." Her voice cracked. "And that's not fair—for either of us."

The city's call to prayer echoed in the distance, haunting and beautiful. Maggy stood, brushing crumbs from her jeans, steeling herself. She reached up, cupping Jean's cheek, her thumb tracing a silent goodbye. "I need to leave, Jean. For both of us. You have to find your way back to yourself—and I need to figure out who I am when I'm not living through you."

He wanted to argue, to ask her to stay, but the words caught in his throat. All he could do was nod, blinking back tears.

Maggy smiled through her pain. "You'll win again, Jean. Maybe not today, maybe not tomorrow. But you will. And when you do, I hope you know it wasn't because of me. It'll be because you remembered who you are." She pressed a fleeting kiss to his forehead, then turned and walked away, her silhouette swallowed by the golden dusk.

For a long moment, Jean stayed at the wall, watching the city lights flicker on across the water. He let the ache settle—of loss, of endings, of the bittersweet truth that loving someone sometimes meant letting them go.

He thought of Maggy's words, of the way she'd tried to protect him from the weight of expectation, the way she'd cared for him not as a competitor, but as a person. The suspicion that she'd come for the fame or the food faded, replaced by something softer—gratitude, and sorrow, and the knowledge that they'd both been undone by something bigger than the contest.

The city's night began to settle, the air cool and fresh. Jean wandered back through the festival streets, alone amidst the crowds. He watched as Dave Snapps accepted congratulations, the new champion surrounded by admirers, but their cheers sounded distant, muffled.

Tonight, Jean nursed two losses: the trophy, and Maggy. But as he walked, he found a measure of peace—knowing that what he'd shared with Maggy was real, and that sometimes, love meant stepping aside so the other could grow. The contest was over, but his journey—both as a competitor, and as a man—was just beginning.

Chapter 9: Cooking Skills Enhanced

A year had passed since the golden dusk when Maggy walked away and Jean stood, heart aching, amid the festival's fading lights. Time, as it does, pressed forward, and Jean found himself caught in the current of competitive cooking—no longer the reigning champion, but far from forgotten. The circuit demanded resilience: each contest another chance to prove his worth, to test his mettle not just against others, but against the echoes of his own legend.

Jean's hands grew stronger, his knife work more precise, his palate sharper with every event. Yet, a quiet loneliness lingered, an absence that colored each victory with a tinge of melancholy. He collected wins—enough to keep the sponsors calling, enough to pay the mortgage on his small apartment overlooking the river—but the joy was muted, like tasting a dish with a missing spice. It was not the loss of the title that haunted him most, but the emptiness in the space where Maggy's encouragement once lived.

In the early days of separation, Jean tried to convince himself that he was fine. He attended cooking demonstrations, filmed short segments for television, and hosted late-night dinners with fellow chefs, all the while projecting an air of confidence. But alone, he struggled. The apartment was too quiet; the city's festival nights blurred into a monotony of lights and fleeting applause. Sometimes, in the hush after a win, he'd catch himself looking for her in the crowd—a flash of auburn hair, a familiar smile—but Maggy was nowhere to be found.

The season turned, and Jean found solace in routine. He woke early, trained relentlessly, and filled notebooks with flavor pairings and plating sketches. His dishes grew bolder—smoked mackerel with charred leeks, spiced lamb with apricot glaze—but he worried they lacked the spark that had once set him apart. He remembered Maggy's words: "You'll win again, Jean… when you remember who you are." He wondered if he'd ever truly known.

It was on a brisk evening in late autumn, as Jean prepared for the qualifying rounds of the world championship, that Maggy returned.

He was in the test kitchen, brow furrowed over a sauce that refused to come together, when he heard the door open behind him. He didn't turn—customers sometimes wandered in by mistake—but the silence that followed was different. Expectant. He looked up and saw her.

Maggy stood in the doorway, windswept and changed, but still unmistakably herself: determined gaze, hands in her pockets, the faintest hint of a nervous smile. For a heartbeat, neither spoke. The memories between them—the sorrow, the longing, the unfinished sentences—hung in the air.

"Hi, Jean," she said, voice softer, yet steadier than he remembered.

He set his whisk down, forcing a smile. "You came back."

Maggy nodded, stepping into the warm glow of the kitchen. "I had to. I needed time. To figure out who I am when I'm not living through you." She let out a shaky breath. "But I missed this. Missed us. And I realized there's still something left to finish."

A part of Jean wanted to close the distance, to reach for her hand—but he stayed where he was, uncertain. "The championship," he said, the weight of the word filling the space between them.

Maggy's smile grew. "Yes, and more than that. I want to help you find your way—not back to who you were, but forward. If you'll let me."

They stood in the kitchen, the hum of the refrigerator the only sound. Then, as if pulled by some unspoken agreement, they moved together—side by side once more, transformed by all they'd endured apart.

Their first training session was awkward at first. Jean, used to solitude, hesitated under Maggy's keen observation. Maggy, for her part, treaded carefully—her coaching less directive, more collaborative, as if she, too, was finding her footing anew.

But as days passed, old rhythms returned, now tempered by humility and mutual respect. They spoke honestly about the pain of their separation, about the ways they'd both lost sight of themselves in the glare of competition and expectation. Maggy admitted her fear: "I thought pushing you to win was enough. But I forgot you're not just a competitor—you're a person. I'm sorry I lost sight of that." Jean, voice quiet, shared his regret at letting their partnership falter. "I wanted to win for us. Not just for the trophy. I think I needed you more than I realized."

The city outside was unchanged—still vibrant, still alive—but within the kitchen, something new was growing. Forgiveness. Trust.

Together, Jean and Maggy set their sights on the world championship. This time, their approach was different: less about relentless perfection, more about rediscovering joy in the craft. Maggy brought with her a journal filled with notes—techniques she'd learned during her time apart, strategies observed in international kitchens, exercises designed to probe both skill and spirit.

"We're not just training your hands," she told Jean one morning as they tasted a new sauce. "We're training your mind. Your heart. The part that cooks not for the judges, but for yourself."

Maggy introduced Jean to methods he'd only read about. Blindfolded taste tests sharpened his palate, forcing him to trust his instincts rather than his eyes. She set up a series of stress drills: surprise ingredient swaps, timed plating challenges, mock interviews with local journalists. At first, Jean chafed under the new routines, his old anxieties resurfacing. But Maggy's feedback was gentle, guiding— never critical, always constructive.

One afternoon, she challenged him to reinvent a dish he'd made hundreds of times: his signature duck confit. "But this time," she said, "make it tell your story. Not mine. Not the judges'. Yours."

Jean hesitated, then went to work. He layered flavors from his childhood—tangy cherries, wild thyme, a hint of smoky paprika reminiscent of his grandmother's old kitchen. When he plated the dish, Maggy tasted it and smiled, tears shining in her eyes. "That's you," she whispered. "That's the Jean I believed in."

Their partnership, once defined by ambition and unspoken longing, began to shift. Jean learned to separate his self-worth from the outcome of each contest. Maggy, too, let go of her need to control every detail, embracing the messy, unpredictable process of true mentorship.

They laughed more, argued less. When setbacks came—a botched sauce, a failed soufflé—they faced them together, analyzing what went wrong, celebrating what went right. In the quiet moments between training, they talked not just about food, but about dreams, regrets, hopes for the future.

Gradually, Jean's confidence returned—not the brash certainty of his early days, but a deeper, steadier belief. He no longer cooked to prove himself to Maggy or anyone else; he cooked because it was who he was. And in that acceptance, he found freedom.

As the world championship approached, Jean was no longer the man who'd watched Maggy's silhouette fade into the dusk. He stood taller, his movements more assured, his creativity unleashed. In the final stretch of training, Maggy unveiled her last set of techniques—visualization, mindful breathing, ways to steady his nerves in the chaos of competition.

On the eve of the contest, Maggy found Jean sitting quietly on the balcony, overlooking the city's glittering lights. She joined him, their hands brushing, silent understanding passing between them.

"Whatever happens tomorrow," she said, "you've already won. You found your way back—to yourself, to your craft, to us."

Jean smiled, peace settling in his chest. "We did," he replied. "Together."

The morning of the world championship dawned bright and clear. Jean entered the arena not as a lone contender, but as half of a partnership forged in adversity and renewed in trust. Maggy watched from the sidelines, pride glowing in her eyes—not just for the competitor he'd become, but for the man.

As Jean plated his final dish, the crowd hushed, anticipation thick in the air. Whatever the judges decided, Jean knew he had already reclaimed something more important than a title: his passion, his purpose, his partnership with Maggy. And in that moment, surrounded by the warmth of shared hope, Jean realized his journey was only just beginning.

Chapter 10: The New Winner

In this chapter Jean enters the world championship contest, the title is named the rooster Muncher Champion Title. Jean will be eating Horny Rooster Dogs and a lot of them to win. If he wins this, he will be world Champion and guess who is in it, yes you guessed it, Dave Snapps. They battle it out with Maggy Cheering and Jeering all the way. Jean wins and takes the title and throws up in the bathroom again, this was some unusual food and he wasn't ready for the taste, Maggy told Jean," it tastes like chicken."

Chapter 10: The New Winner

The sun crept up over the city, its rays spilling gold across the rooftops and flooding into Jean's modest hotel room. Somewhere down the hallway, a blender whirred— someone was up early, prepping for glory or perhaps just making a protein shake. But Jean was awake long before the alarm, mind racing faster than a sous-chef on a Saturday night.

This was no ordinary morning. This was the day of the World Championship, the infamous Horny Cock Muncher Champion Title. The title itself sounded like something out of a cartoon, but Jean knew better. It was the Holy Grail of competitive eating—a test of stomach, willpower, and questionable life choices.

He stared at his reflection and tried to look confident. Instead, his face looked back with the wide-eyed panic of a man who'd just realized what, exactly, "Horny Rooster Dogs" entailed. He'd heard legends: part sausage, part mystery meat, all bravado. A dish so infamous that even the bravest contestants had bowed out, clutching their midsections and whispering silent prayers to the gods of digestion.

Maggy, unfazed as ever, leaned on the hotel balcony, sipping coffee. She held her mug like a trophy, steam curling around her smile. "Ready?" she asked with a glint of mischief.

"As I'll ever be," Jean replied, though his voice cracked a little on the last word. He wondered if nerves ever just, you know, took a day off.

The competition hall was decked out like a carnival fever dream. Neon signs blinked overhead: Welcome, Rooster

Munchers! A ten-foot inflatable rooster bobbed near the entrance, eyes wild and beak open in a silent scream. Somewhere, an announcer was already hyping up the crowd, his voice echoing through the rafters.

Jean's competitors milled about: men and women of various shapes and sizes, each with a gleam in their eye and stretchy pants cinched tight. But all eyes kept drifting toward the reigning champion—Dave Snapps, the man, the myth, the legend. Dave stood by his table, flexing his jaw like a boxer warming up, his presence as intimidating as his Instagram feed.

Maggy elbowed Jean gently. "Remember the breathing. And if you see Dave doing that weird eyebrow thing, just ignore him."

Jean nodded, clutching his lucky spatula (not that he'd need it, but it had been with him through worse). The emcee called for contestants to take their places. Heart pounding,

Jean stepped forward, greeted by the deafening roar of the crowd and a waft of spicy, meaty air that made his stomach do a cautious backflip.

The rules were simple. In front of each competitor sat a mountain—no, a geological formation—of Horny Rooster Dogs: bun, mystery meat, a dash of something that looked like relish but smelled like vengeance. Consume as many as possible in thirty minutes. No utensils, no mercy, no second thoughts.

Maggy cheered from the sidelines, her voice cutting through the chaos. "Let's go, Jean! Show those roosters who's boss!" A few fans picked up the chant, though several just looked confused, probably wondering what a rooster dog actually was.

The starting horn blared—a sound not unlike a rooster deciding it was done with life. Hands shot out. Rooster Dogs vanished. Sausage flew. Jean tried to pace himself, but soon realized "pacing" was for amateurs. Dave Snapps, two seats down, was inhaling food with mechanical precision, his count already in the double digits.

Jean dug in. The first bite: salty, spicy, and faintly reminiscent of something his grandmother once tried to feed the family cat. Still, he pressed on, channeling every lesson Maggy had drilled into him—visualization, mindful chewing, and, above all, trying not to imagine where the "horny" part came in.

Time blurred. Jean's world shrank to the platter in front of him. Competitors dropped out, one by one, some clutching their stomachs, others just staring at the sky, asking silent questions of the universe. Jean kept going. When the count reached thirty, he paused, sweat beading on his forehead.

Dave Snapps caught his eye, flashed a cocky grin, and wolfed down three more in a row. The crowd went wild.

Maggy jeered back, "Come on Dave, don't choke!" The announcer thought it was hilarious.

With the final seconds ticking away, Jean felt the room spin—a heady blend of adrenaline, sodium, and sheer disbelief at how much he'd consumed—yet he refused to yield, matching Dave bite for bite until, at the sound of the closing buzzer, he crammed in one last defiant mouthful and slammed his hands on the table, victorious and gasping.

Silence fell as the tally began, and when the emcee declared Jean the new Horne Cock Muncher Champion, the crowd erupted in cheers and laughter; Maggy raced forward, wrapping him in a triumphant hug despite his protests that he might actually explode. As confetti cannons boomed and camera flashes stung his eyes, Jean fought a losing battle with his queasy stomach, dashing for the restroom amid the chorus of celebration, but even as he emptied the spoils of victory, he grinned—because this,

bizarre as it was, felt like a beginning, not just for his title,

but for the life he and Maggy would savor together, one

improbable challenge at a time.

Note from the Author

To You,

I would like to thank all of you, the readers, and all of you,

the family, for your support and yearning to read.

With gratitude,

Willie S.

www.ingramcontent.com/pod-product-compliance
Lightning Source LLC
Chambersburg PA
CBHW071414170626
46811CB00003B/1403